NEW YEAR'S DAY

NEW YEAR'S DAY

MONICA MURPHY

Copyright © 2023 by Monica Murphy

All rights reserved.

No part of this book may be reproduced in any form or by any electronic or mechanical means, including information storage and retrieval systems, without written permission from the author, except for the use of brief quotations in a book review.

This book is a work of fiction. Names, characters, places, and incidents are used fictitiously. Any resemblance to actual persons, living or dead, events, or locales, is entirely coincidental.

Cover design: Emily Wittig
emilywittigdesigns.com

Proofreader: Sarah, All Encompassing Books

To the readers, especially the Swifties.

Here's to holding on to the memories.

PLAYLIST

"New Year's Day" - Taylor Swift
"NYE" - Local Natives, Suki Waterhouse
"IRIS" - Ashes to Amber
"'tis the damn season" - Taylor Swift
"Valentine" - Current Blue, STEPHAN
"Lookaround" - Edgehill
"Natural" - Shelly

Find the **NEW YEAR'S DAY** playlist here: https://bit.ly/3R5oh4k

Or scan the QR code below:

ONE
WILLOW

NEW YEAR'S *Eve*

"Ready?" Iris asks. I swear her body is vibrating with excitement.

Mine is too.

I nod at my cousin, the both of us smiling at each other before I reach for the handle and slowly open the door. The slight creak of the hinges has us both frozen for a second, but the music coming from downstairs drowns out any other sound.

We're in the clear.

"Let's go," Iris whispers as she darts out of her bedroom first.

I sneak out after her, slowly closing the door and heading for the meeting spot we all agreed upon earlier.

The entire family is here to celebrate the New Year at the estate where August, Iris and Vaughn's parents now live. It's close to the ocean and there are so many rooms, I get lost in here every time we come to visit, which is often.

Makes me grateful for our more normal sized home back in the city. My dad keeps trying to convince Mom we need to move out here or at the very least to a neighborhood just like this, but Mom refuses.

"I love the city too much to leave it," she's told him more than once.

I always silently agree with her. And Daddy always gives in to her wishes. I love spending time here, but I prefer the city too.

Iris and I approach the landing, not surprised at all to find August waiting there along with my brother, Rowan. Their already bored expressions match, and even though I'm two years older than Row, he's almost as grumpy as August. Or he's just imitating him because he looks up to August so much.

I mean, how cynical can you be when you're ten?

"Are we really going to sit here and watch our parents drink, dance and make out?" August grimaces, shaking his head. "That sounds like a nightmare."

"I want to see what they're wearing." The women in my family always dress up for New Year's Eve. You can always count on seeing vivid colors and an overabundance of sparkles. Iris and I can't wait to be old someday and dress like they do.

Tonight the boys are still in jeans or khakis and sweaters, but us girls decided to dress up too, wearing our favorite dresses.

"Me too." Iris walks right up to where her brother sits cross-legged in front of the balustrade, kicking him with her bare foot.

He doesn't even flinch. "If you don't like it, go do something else."

"There's nothing else to do." August yawns and I send Iris a look, but she's not paying attention.

She finds her big brother so annoying and I get it. He's always acting too cool to spend time with us.

"Yeah." Row also yawns and I roll my eyes. "This is boring."

"Shut up," I tell him, feeling mean the moment the words leave me. I plop down next to him on the floor. "Sorry," I whisper, leaning my head on his narrow shoulder but he pulls away, annoyed with me.

"Whatever." Row shrugs, sending me a quick, grateful look. I can't keep up the mean sister act like Iris can. I'm too nice and I never want to hurt someone's feelings. Daddy says I'm just like Mom, who's kind to everyone and I guess he's right. Even though sometimes inside, I do feel mean.

What sounds like a herd of elephants make their way toward us, all of them spilling out of the various bedrooms, their chatter louder than it should be. August and Iris's youngest brother Vaughn leads the pack and he stops, holding out his arms to block the rest of them from going any further.

"Quiet guys," he commands and they do as he asks.

I'm impressed that an eight-year-old can get the rest of the cousins—who are all the same age as Vaughn—to do as he says. I study them all, my little brother Beau standing with the rest of them. They include Christopher, who is Spencer and Sylvie's only son. And then there's Carolina and West's twin daughters, Paris and Pru.

"Come on." Iris waves her hand. "You can all sit here."

They walk over to us in a line, all of them settling in front of the railing, their hands going to the spindles, curling around them as they stare down at the party unfolding below.

The butler—who's been with the family for ages and we all adore him for sneaking us candy—is patiently waiting by the door with his hands behind his back, his worried gaze occasionally going to one of the windows that flanks either side of the massive door. I can see what he's watching from my perch on the second landing. It's the snow.

It's coming down in buckets.

There are candles lit everywhere and music plays from the speakers that are placed discreetly throughout the house. Right now, it's a gentle piano playing a familiar tune, but later on they'll put on the more current hits, when everyone drinks champagne and dances with big smiles on their faces.

Someday I will be doing the same thing with my cousins and I can't wait.

"Look at her dress," Iris breathes, pressing her face between the spindles, her gaze stuck on her Aunt Sylvie, who is wearing a formfitting dress covered in iridescent sequins. "I love it."

"It's beautiful," I agree but I'm not ready to think it's my favorite of the night. I need to see everyone else first.

We've done this for the last couple of years on New Year's Eve. The parents put us to bed—but they know none of us actually go to sleep. Eventually we'll make our way down the stairs and sneak into the kitchen where Marta the housekeeper will serve us some appetizers and desserts from the party that she saved just for us. We'll drink sparkling cider in the special glasses used for champagne only and say cheers to each other. We pretend we're at the party too until we eventually head back upstairs and watch them some more.

It's all very glamorous and exciting to us girls. The boys claim they don't care about any of it, but they never manage to find something else to do on this night so I think secretly they must like it.

I know I love it. Someday I'll be with the adults at the party, and a new generation of children will be watching. Maybe even my children.

A sigh leaves me and I wonder if I'll ever be a mother. I'll have to fall in love first I suppose, but what if I don't? I can still be a mother. I could adopt.

But I want to fall in love. Seeing my parents together and how much they love each other is inspiring. My father is just as romantic as my mother, maybe even more so and that is just the sweetest.

Now, I do have crushes on boys all the time, but my mind is constantly changing. I can't stick with just one boy long enough to develop any real feelings, but my mom says I'm too young and I shouldn't focus on any one boy anyway.

I guess she's right and besides, it's kind of fun to focus on a variety of boys...

"Your mom looks beautiful," Iris murmurs, nudging her shoulder against mine.

I smile, admiring how gorgeous she is in the red dress she already showed me earlier. She does look beautiful. People say I look like her, but I just don't see it. Doesn't help that I've got braces on my teeth and I'm flat-chested. Wren Lancaster is the farthest thing from flat-chested and she's just so elegant in everything she wears. It's how she carries herself too. I'd give anything to truly look like her someday. "She does."

"My mom does too." The despair on my cousin's face is almost alarming. "I will never look like her. I don't care what my father says."

"You already do." I pat her knee, trying to reassure her. "And I was just having the same thought. I don't look anything like my mother."

The two glamorous women are standing in the foyer, talking to the butler in low murmurs, their brows drawing together in matching expressions of concern.

"Crew," Mom calls, her voice full of alarm. "Could you come here, please?"

My father appears seconds later, standing at my mother's side, his hand settled low on her back. He's listening to the butler I assume repeat what he said to Mom and Summer, and Iris and I both have our heads tilted forward, hoping to catch what is being said.

But all I can hear is the dumb piano tinkling.

Whit appears seconds later, demanding to know what's happening and the butler fills him in as well.

"Something is going on," Iris tells me, her voice hushed and her Lancaster blue eyes extra wide. "You realize no guests have shown up yet."

Iris is right. No one has arrived and that's unusual considering the time. "Do you think it's because of the snow?"

"Probably." Iris nods, her expression now crestfallen. "I hope they don't cancel the party."

"I hope they do. It's so boring." August makes snoring noises and Row laughs. A little too loudly, which of course catches the attention of both sets of parents.

Oh no.

They all four glance up at the landing at the same time, our mothers exchanging a knowing smile with each other before Summer starts heading up the stairs.

She's not my aunt but she feels like one—Whit is Daddy's cousin. Our parents are all so close and I love it. My dad is close to his siblings as well but not all of them are here tonight. My uncle Grant and his wife are currently in Switzerland and Aunt Charlotte and Uncle Perry are in the city, spending the holiday with their immediate family.

Summer pauses at the top of the stairs, her hand resting on the railing. The light catches on the massive diamond on her finger and I wonder if it's new. I've never seen it before.

"What are you children doing?" Her tone is teasing and we all know she isn't angry.

And she also knows exactly what we're doing.

"Spying on you!" is what Vaughn tells her as he leaps to his feet and runs to her, wrapping his arms around her legs and tilting his head back to smile at his mom. "You look pretty."

"Why thank you." She ruffles his dark hair that matches hers, a faint smile still on her face as she glances up and takes in the rest of us. "Well, the terrible weather seems to have closed the roads and none of our guests can make it to the party tonight."

"Does that mean we get to eat all the food?" Row asks hopefully. He's always hungry lately. Dad says he's growing and warns that someday he'll be taller than me.

I can't imagine it but I know what my father says will most likely be true.

August slaps my brother's arm. "Have a little class, cousin."

Iris rolls her eyes. "Right, because you're sooooo classy, Augie."

He sends his younger sister a death glare. "Better watch what you say, Iris, or—"

"Enough." Summer's gentle but firm tone silences her squabbling children. "I do think we're going to have plenty of food to take care of your healthy appetite, Rowan."

My brother's cheeks turn red and he ducks his head.

"Looks like the New Year's Eve party is family only this evening!" Summer laughs when we all start to cheer. "Consider this your official invite."

"Wait a minute." I jump to my feet, my gaze going to Mom who's currently walking up the stairs, stopping right next to Summer. "We get to come to the party tonight?"

Mom nods. "We have all of this food and decorations and music playing. We can't let it go to waste just because of some snow."

"Come on." Summer hooks her arm through Mom's and they both start walking down the stairs. We all trail after them. "Let's get this party started!"

TWO
WHIT

I WATCH Summer and Wren lead our children into the front living room, where we've chosen to hold our annual New Year's Eve party for the last couple of years. When I was a child, my parents had the party in the grand ballroom. Hundreds of people would come every year—it was a much-anticipated party by the social set. My parents went all out with the food and drink and entertainment.

Eventually when their marriage was in trouble, my mother—God rest her damaged soul—would use the party as a weapon, spending as much money on it as she possibly could. My father would retaliate by fucking a random party guest in a bathroom or closet, hoping Mother would find him.

My parents were a disaster together. I vowed to myself—and to my wife when I married her—that I would never do that. Besides, I'm too obsessed with Summer to even think about anyone else.

I also couldn't give two fucks about New York's high society and having them in my home for a bullshit party to ring in the new year. I much prefer inviting my family and real, actual friends to celebrate with. Who wants to schmooze with a bunch of phony assholes?

Not me.

"Darling, would you please change the music?" Summer asks me with a sweet smile on her face.

I flash her a wolfish grin and pull out my phone, scrolling through the various playlists we've created over the years. "Of course, darling. Coming right up."

We call each other darling in front of the kids because it sounds nice. We know how to be proper in front of children and mixed company. Behind closed doors though?

We're still pretty goddamn wild when it comes to...fucking.

I choose a playlist full of songs I know every one of my three children will find something to like, even August, and turn up the volume. The music fills the room, the younger children all screaming their excitement loud enough to make me wince. They run to the middle of the room and start dancing, looking absolutely ridiculous as they shuffle their feet and wiggle their bodies, but they're having the time of their lives.

And the party has barely begun.

After a few minutes of discussing food matters with Marta our housekeeper, Summer approaches me. I reach for her, slipping my arm around her slender waist, my fingers settling on the bare skin of her back. Her dress is made of soft black velvet and covers most of her body with the exception of her back.

Very chic, my wife. And extremely sexy.

"Is it wrong to say I'm not sad that our original guests can't make it because of a snowstorm?" Summer tilts her head toward me, resting it on my shoulder for a moment. I catch her scent and my dick twitches.

The timing is all wrong, but maybe we could sneak off later and I can fuck her in a coat closet or something. God knows we have enough closets in this monstrosity of a house.

"No, it's not wrong." I tighten my hold on her and pull her in closer. "Looks like our new party goers are already having a great time."

"They are." Her smile is wistful. "I adore them."

"They're a wild bunch," I say in agreement, because they are. And I adore them as well, especially our own.

"They're all getting so big." Her voice is full of sadness, my least favorite thing of all time. There is nothing I wouldn't do to ease my wife's melancholy.

Thank God it doesn't happen too often.

"They are."

"August is...a lot." She sighs, her gaze lifting to mine. "And I think we're raising some well-adjusted children."

I chuckle and press my lips to her forehead in the briefest kiss. "He's a Lancaster and the oldest male. His shitty attitude comes naturally."

"His attitude isn't shitty, he's just so..." Her voice drifts.

"Judgmental?" I raise my brows. "Thinks he's above it all? Sounds familiar."

"This family name sometimes feels like a curse," she murmurs, her brows drawing together with worry.

"It's not a curse." This time I kiss her lips, savoring the sweet taste of her. "We've changed the course of every one of these children's lives in this room right now. Look how happy they are. Look at Christopher."

My sister Sylvie's son is laughing and smiling, having fun with his cousins. The fact that she's a mother still shocks me and she's been one for a while now. This was a girl who was abused by our mother. Who stated quite loudly and as many times as she could that she would never be a mom.

Now she is, and she's a good one too. Christopher is the same age as our youngest Vaughn and they're extremely close.

"He looks like Spencer," Summer murmurs and I nod my agreement.

"And look at Carolina's children." The twins are wearing matching sparkly gold dresses, their blonde hair pulled into high ponytails. "Carolina used to hate people. She especially hated all of us."

My gaze goes to Carolina who's standing with her husband West on the other side of the room near the fireplace. They look happy. No, even better, they seem content.

Growing up, none of us were able to feel content for any length of time. Not with our overbearing mother and rarely present father. Too bad he's not here to witness this, but he's currently in the Bahamas with his latest girlfriend—who is younger than Carolina—ringing in the New Year on his yacht.

Some things just never change, and I can't blame my father for that. He tried the best he could. He's made up for a lot of his bad behavior from the past these last few years. We're closer than ever, and he spends a lot of time with my children. With all of our children.

It's the least he can do. I draw the line at him bringing his girlfriends around the children, though. Since they're interchangeable, what's the point?

"You're right," Summer says, her voice drawing me out of my thoughts. "I shouldn't say it's a curse. Our generation has changed the Lancaster attitude for the better."

"Indeed, it has." I tuck her close, pressing my lips to her cheek before I fully kiss her on the lips.

"Daddy!" I feel a tug on the back of my suit jacket and I pull away from my wife's irresistible lips to find our daughter watching us with an imploring gaze.

"What's wrong?" I ask her, turning so both Summer and I can face Iris.

She is the spitting image of her mother, though she's in that awkward preteen phase where it feels like she's all limbs and awkward with it. She's also constantly running into things, as if she's unable to control herself. Summer said she was the same way and I can't even imagine it. "I think August snuck a glass of champagne."

My gaze cuts to the bar where I see my oldest son standing in front of it, sipping from a glass that looks very much like champagne.

"And he gave one to Row," Iris whispers. "Who's only ten."

"Oh dear." Summer pulls away from me, her expression full of alarm. "I'll go talk to him."

She's gone in an instant, leaving behind a very pleased looking little sister who just ratted on her brother.

"Thank you for telling us." My voice is firm, my gaze locking on my sweet daughter's beautiful face. "But can I—warn you about something?"

"Yes, Daddy." She nods, her eyes wide.

Bending down, I get on her level, reaching out to cup her soft cheek, cradling the side of her face for a brief moment. "No one likes a snitch, sweetheart."

She blinks at me. "What do you mean?"

"Just…don't tell on your big brother every chance you get, especially as you get older. He's an ally, not your enemy." My hand drops from her face and I rise to my full height, Iris tilting her head back, watching me with a confused expression on her face.

"If he's doing something bad, shouldn't I tell you about it?"

"Well…yes." Being a parent is complicated sometimes, Jesus. "But he's your brother. And you need to stick together with your brothers. As you get older, you're going to need them in your life. You'll value that relationship because no one knows what it's like to be you—what it was like, growing up in your household. Only your brothers will truly understand."

Iris wrinkles her nose. "They're boys. They're totally different than me. And look at him. He's drinking champagne and he's only fifteen!"

She sounds outraged, which makes me smother the laugh that wants to escape with my hand. "There's no harm in it. Not really. We're at home. He's surrounded by family. One glass isn't going to ruin him forever."

I think of a time when I drank champagne with a certain beautiful fourteen-year-old and I was completely enchanted by her. The moment I met Summer, it was as if lightning struck me where I stood. I was electrified, never the same again.

And look at us now. Married with three children. I wouldn't change this life for anything. Summer is without a doubt the one for me. Just like I'm the one for her.

Iris is gaping at me, shocked I would say such a thing. "What if *I* had a glass of champagne?"

"You're too young."

"But Row had one."

"And now it's gone." I turn to look at the bar to see Wren with the glass of champagne in her hand, Row standing beside her wearing a sullen look on his face. I turn to study my daughter once more. I'm glad I only have one girl. I love her and am terribly protective of her but if there were two?

I would be a mess.

"Augie doesn't like me." Iris crosses her arms, a pout on her pretty face. "He's always telling me to leave him alone. He never wants to spend time with me."

"Well, he'll never want to spend time with you if you're constantly telling on him," I point out.

Iris drops her arms at her sides, pursing her lips. "That makes sense."

"I know." I tap my temple with my index finger. "I'm a smart guy sometimes."

She laughs, launching herself at me and I wrap her up in a hug. "You're a smart guy all the time. I love you."

I squeeze her close, cherishing her sweet hugs. Her sweeter words. "I love you too, my pretty little flower."

Iris tilts her head back and I bop her nose with my index finger, making her laugh. "I'm going to go talk to August. Maybe he'll be nice to me."

"You tell him I said he has to be nice to you," I say sternly.

She rolls her eyes. "But won't that make him hate me more if I told him that?"

So logical, my girl. "Yes. You're probably right."

"I'm just going to act cool. Like I wasn't the one who got Row in trouble." Iris pulls out of my arms and they immediately feel empty. "Bye."

I watch her head for her brother, my wife returning by my side and my chest suddenly aches.

"I hate that they have to grow up," I murmur.

Summer leans her head against my shoulder, a sigh leaving her. "I hate it too. Why can't they stay little forever?"

"Because we can't fuck around in the house behind closed doors forever," I say with a faint snicker.

Summer lightly slaps my chest. "You're bad."

I dip my head, my lips right at her ear. "You love it."

A sigh escapes her just before I kiss her. "I do."

THREE
CREW

"CHAMPAGNE, SON? REALLY?" I stare at the top of my oldest son's head, which is currently bent downward. Rowan can't face me and I understand why.

He's sipping on champagne snagged for him by his fifteen-year-old shitty cousin.

Okay, August isn't shitty but he's so like his father it's not even funny. Which means he's...

Damn it, he's a little shitty.

"August said it would be fun," Row says to the floor. "But I thought it tasted awful."

Good, is what I want to say, but I restrain myself.

"Do you believe everything that August tells you?" When it comes to my children, I try my best to have patience. Sometimes, I get angry. I am definitely the bad guy in the parental situation and Wren is almost always the good guy. Which I have no problem with, though it's hard for me to be tough on my daughter.

Willow just has to look at me with those big beautiful eyes of hers, her lips forming into a pout and I'm a goner. I'd probably let her get away with murder and take the fall for it. She's got me wrapped tight around her finger.

But Rowan? I rarely have to discipline him. He's a pretty good kid. Both of my boys are.

This is all August's fault.

"I won't ever do it again." Row lifts his head, his glassy gaze meeting mine and I realize he's this close to bursting into tears. And we can't have that. Not tonight, when we're celebrating New Year's Eve. "I'm sorry."

"Come here," I say, my voice rough as I pull him into my arms and give him a quick hug. He springs away from me fast, glancing around. Probably doesn't want to get caught being comforted by his dad in front of August. "Don't do it again."

"Do what?" Row frowns.

"Drink alcohol. You're ten years old for Christ's sake." I shake my head, rubbing the side of my jaw with my hand. "At least wait until you're in high school."

Row frowns. "Did you drink alcohol when you were in high school?"

This being a parent thing is tricky business.

"Sometimes," I hedge.

"Oh." Row nods, watching the rest of his cousins at the buffet table laden with food. His eyes are full of longing, and knowing my child, he's starving.

He always is.

"Go get something to eat," I tell him and he doesn't even look back.

No, Row dashes off, standing with the rest of his cousins who are all younger than him save for his sister, Iris and August. Rowan just wants them to accept him but he's considered younger and therefore, they're dismissive of him all the time.

It's frustrating for him. That's why he's drinking champagne when he's ten. He's just trying to keep up.

Shaking my head, I'm about to march over to Whit and let him know my real feelings about his son when I feel a gentle hand land on my arm, keeping me from moving.

"Did you punish him?"

I glance to my right to find my wife standing there, her delicate brows drawn together, her lips forming into the slightest frown. She looks upset. It's not every day you discover that your ten-year-old is trying to sample champagne.

At least it wasn't tequila.

"I didn't punish him." I shrug, wondering if I should've. "I just told him it was completely out of line and he's too young. He's only ten for the love of God. Oh, and I blame August for convincing him to try it."

"August is very...pushy sometimes," Wren murmurs. "And all Row wants is to earn August's approval. He'll do anything to gain it."

That was me with my brothers. I idolized them and they were complete and utter dicks toward me most of the time. Being the baby of the family sucks. "I've been in his position before."

"And you turned out just fine." She's smiling as she steps closer, her arms going around me so she can clutch me close. "Look at you."

"My brothers were dicks," I admit, studying her beautiful face. All these years later and she's still just as gorgeous as when I first saw her. Maybe even more so.

"Sometimes they still are." Her smile grows and then she's laughing. "Oh, they're the worst. But I miss them this year."

"I miss them as well." They're celebrating with their own families, not wanting to make the trek out here, which worked out for them considering the snowstorm. "Don't forget that Whit can be pretty bad too."

"He's terrible," she agrees with a grin. "But I love him. And he loves his family more than anything else, which counters any of his bad qualities."

"I love my family too." I kiss her because I can't resist my Birdy. "We're going to have to keep Willow under lock and key when she becomes a teenager."

My gaze goes to our only daughter, who is currently laughing over something Iris said to her. Those two adore each other and I'm glad Willow has a cousin to always hang out with when we have these family get togethers. So does our youngest son, Beau. But poor Rowan?

He's the odd man out.

"Willow," I suddenly call. My daughter turns her head in our direction. "Come here for a second."

"What are you up to?" Wren asks but I just flash her a quick smile.

Willow whispers something to Iris before she makes her way over to us, nibbling on a bacon wrapped shrimp. "Is everything okay?"

"I wanted to ask you a question," I start but Willow cuts me off.

"No, I didn't try any of the champagne." She stands a little taller, her nose tilted in the air. "I wouldn't dare."

I send a quick look to Wren, wondering if she's seeing what I'm seeing.

She is truly her mother's daughter.

"I didn't think you did," I reassure her, noting how her shoulders relax a little at my words. "I was hoping you could include your brother tonight."

"Include him how?"

"Well, you're always with Iris. Why don't you let Rowan hang out with the two of you. He'd love it."

"No." She shakes her head.

"Willow," Wren chastises. "Don't be like that."

"He'll ruin everything," Willow whines. "Iris and I like it better when it's just the two of us."

"But you exclude everyone else," Wren explains. "And your brother is a little down in the dumps tonight."

"Why, because he got caught drinking champagne and he's only ten?" Willow rolls her eyes.

"Yes, that's part of it. But he's always trying to keep up with August and he's too young." Wren reaches out and rests her hand on Willow's shoulder, giving it a gentle squeeze. "Spend a little time with your brother tonight. Make him feel like he's a part of something."

"Why doesn't he hang out with Beau and Vaughn and the rest of the them?"

"They're younger than him," I start but Willow is already shaking her head.

"And he's younger than me," she oh so kindly reminds us.

"Willow, just—be a good sister and spend some time with Row," I tell her, tamping down the faint irritation that's rising. "He just wants to be included."

"Fine," Willow says with an exasperated breath.

I pull her into me before she can stomp off, giving her a hug. "Don't forget to come give me a kiss at midnight."

Our daughter gazes up at me, her lips curved in the faintest smile. "You know all of my kisses are for you, Daddy. And Mama."

I pat the side of her head before she turns and runs away from us. "Rowan! Come over here."

Row scurries over to where the girls are standing, Iris seemingly confused by the new addition to their usual twosome.

Keeping my gaze on Willow, I murmur, "She's growing up so fast, Wren. One day all of her kisses won't be for me anymore."

"You'll always have mine," my wife whispers to me.

I slip my arm around her shoulders, tucking her close to my side. "We still owe each other at least a million."

Wren laughs. "The amount grows every time we talk about it."

I grin. I can't help it. I'm greedy."

"It's a Lancaster trait," she says.

I dip my head, kissing her lips. Always tempted by my wife's sexy mouth.

"You're a good father." She pats my chest.

"Even when I harass and force my children to be nice to each other?"

"Oh, especially then."

"You're a good mom." I kiss her again. "A great one."

Wren slips out from underneath my arm, only to link her arm through mine. "Come on. Let's go drink some champagne and get drunk."

"In front of the children?" I raise my brows, already leading her toward the bar.

"Definitely. We don't know how long we're going to be snowed in with this bunch. We're probably going to need all the liquor we can get," Wren says, her eyes twinkling.

Damn, I didn't even think of that, but that's my wife for you.

Always so wise.

FOUR
SYLVIE

I'M IN A MASSIVE, overstuffed chair with my husband, and I'm sitting on his lap. Spencer has his arms wrapped around me, and they're just the comfort that I need. He knows how I feel about this house and what happened in it. He was there when my mother died here.

Whit refuses to let that incident define this house or our family.

"It was an accident," he stressed to me the last time we talked about it. "Too many generations of Lancasters have passed through these halls. I'm not about to let what happened taint this home forever. I can't. I have a family to raise."

He and Summer have a beautiful family and they're currently raising them in this house. The house where they were married. A house that is full of laughter and joy. Where young children seem to spill out of every room, including my very own.

My son, Christopher.

He's with his cousins who are the same age—Vaughn and Beau. And Pru and Paris, my sister's twins. They're all laughing and stuffing their faces full of food. Mostly desserts. They're so excited that they can party with us—a direct quote from Christopher. They've watched us enjoying our New Year's Eve party for the last few years and now they're an actual part of it.

I don't think I've ever seen them more excited.

"Hey. Are you all right?" Spence murmurs close to my forehead, just before he presses his lips to it in the softest kiss.

Nodding, I lean into him, grateful to be tucked away in this little corner, watching everything unfold. I much prefer being an observer, especially as I get older. "This has turned into a perfect night."

"Being snowed in with your family and all these children?" Spence sounds amused. It might be his own personal form of hell, but he doesn't seem that upset about it.

When is he ever? He's the balm to my soul. The calm to my storm.

"Yes." My voice is firm. "I'm so tired of schmoozing with people I barely know at this party. Spending the last day of the year with my family is the best way to celebrate the old and ring in the new."

"It's going to be a good year." He kisses my cheek this time and I snuggle closer, not caring who can see us. We're still in love.

Every adult in this room is in love with their significant other. It's a beautiful thing to witness, because after dealing with the horrible nightmare that was all of our parents, we're doing things right with this next generation.

I'm proud of it. Proud of us. This is how it should be.

"Hey, Aunt Sylvie. Uncle Spencer." Iris appears in front of the overstuffed chair we're sitting in, aiming a polaroid camera right at us. "I'm going to take your photo. Smile!"

I tilt my head toward Spencer's, a closed-mouth smile on my face as we pose. She hits the button, the flash blinding me for a moment. Spencer laughs, his arms tightening around me.

"Thanks, Iris. Now all I can see is spots," Spencer tells her.

"Sorry." Iris shrugs her slender shoulders, reminding me of a young Summer. "Thanks for the photo! Byeeeee."

She's gone as fast as she appeared, stopping and snapping photos of everyone she runs into. I watch her go, grateful that she's so free and comfortable in this house. In her life. I remember being that age.

I was miserable. Scared.

Sick.

"You get melancholy every time we're in this house," Spencer murmurs to me. "And I hate it."

"I'm sorry." I turn to him, forcing a smile. "Maybe I need some cheering up."

"I've got the perfect solution." He gently pushes me out of his lap and I have no choice but to stand. "We're going to dance."

"Dance?" I'm shocked. "Spencer, you don't really dance."

He has terrible rhythm. It's almost amusing how bad he is.

"I do now. Come on." He stands, taking my hand and leading me to the center of the room where the furniture is already pushed out of the way. "Whit, we need some dance music."

"Dance music?" Carolina asks. "Are we dancing now?"

I send my sister a helpless look, not sure where Spencer is going with this. Usually, we don't start dancing until closer to midnight and when we're full of alcohol. The inhibitions ae loosened and we're a little freer. Able to make fools of ourselves without any worry since we're drunk.

"We are," Spencer says firmly, just as the song switches to one with a faster beat. "Come on, kids. Let's all dance!"

The children join us, their faces full of joy as they start be-bopping all around the room. Whatever they lack in skill they make up with enthusiasm, and I feel myself getting caught up in the pure joy of moving my body and laughing with my family. The song switches to another one, the children screaming their approval and while the lyrics are silly, I can see why the children are loving it.

Even August is dancing with us, although reluctantly. He's too self-conscious, too aware that others might be watching him and oh, how I can relate.

I go to my nephew, stopping directly in front of him and grabbing his hands. He lets me, his smile turning genuine as I swing him around, the both of us spinning so fast the room starts to blur.

Throwing my head back, I laugh and laugh and when we finally slow down, I'm still a little dizzy, stumbling over my feet.

"You okay, Mom?"

I turn to find my beautiful boy in front of me, his expression full of concern. Even a little bit of worry. He's not used to seeing his mother acting like a fool. Or maybe he is.

He might think I'm drunk, though I've only been sipping on a single glass of wine all night.

"I'm great, my sweet." I wrap him up in my arms and hold him close, breathing deep his Christopher scent. This boy of mine is going to turn into a young man soon and I can hardly stand the thought. "How are you? Are you having a good time?"

"This party is fun," he says once I pull away from him. "No wonder you guys have it every year."

"It's usually a lot stuffier and there's not nearly as much dancing," I tell him, which is the truth.

Christopher frowns. "So it's not as fun."

"No." I shake my head. "Being with family is the best part of it all."

He's nodding his agreement, his smile growing. "I agree. And the food."

I laugh. "Yes, and the food."

Spencer is suddenly standing beside me, towering over me as he slides his arm around my shoulders and pulls me into his side. "You two going to dance some more?"

"She danced with August, not me," Christopher points out.

"Then I believe it's your turn next, don't you think?" Spencer glances at me and I nod, reaching out to take our son's hand.

Spencer's arm falls away from me and I take both of my son's hands, spinning around with him much like I did with August. Eventually Vaughn joins us, as well as Carolina's twin girls, and soon we're all turning in a large circle. Every one of us connected, even August.

Even Whit.

I smile at Spencer, who's directly across from me, as we all hold up our linked hands at the end of the song, some of us cheering. But me?

I mouth to my husband, *thank you*.

Spencer always knows exactly what I need.

FIVE
CAROLINA

"I'M TIRED." Paris stretches her arms above her head, delivering a jaw-cracking yawn for emphasis.

I glance at the clock on the wall. "It's just past eleven-thirty. Not much longer to midnight now."

"I don't know if I can make it." Paris rubs her eyes, her sister magically appearing at her side and grabbing one of her hands and tugging on it.

"Come on, Paris. You'll be fine." Pru drags her away from where I stand with West, Paris sending us a glance full of longing over her shoulder before she turns and starts complaining to Pru.

West is shaking his head, chuckling. "We should let Paris go to bed."

"And miss the countdown to midnight? I don't think so." I do a twirl in front of my husband, always wanting to dance but most everyone has settled down, awaiting the clock to strike twelve. The housekeeper brought out a tray full of cups of hot chocolate for the children along with cookies and brownies, and all of the kids—even some of the adults—are eating themselves into a sugar coma.

Even West is nibbling on the corner of a brownie and when he offers it to me, I take a delicate bite, laughing when he shoves more of it into my mouth. I eventually take the whole thing from him and finish it off, licking the tips of my fingers when I do.

"That was a mistake on my part," West says, his gaze zeroed in on my mouth. "Marta's brownies are the best I've ever had."

"It was delicious," I say with relish, acting like a brat because I can.

But only with him.

For some reason I dreaded coming to my brother's house for the annual New Year's Eve party this year. I wanted to stay home, all cozy in our apartment, enjoying the quietness that comes during that week between Christmas and New Year's. The girls were happy staying home as well, playing with their new toys and watching movies at night with us. I didn't want to leave the safety and warmth of our sweet little nest.

It didn't help that the drive to Whit and Summer's was a tad treacherous. The weather was terrible, the snow already coming down in thick white sheets, and West was having a hard time seeing, which made me nervous. By the time we arrived, I was an agitated, nervous wreck, thankful to be here for the next couple of days.

Turns out that getting snowed in and celebrating the New Year with only your immediate family isn't such a bad thing. There's no need for small talk or being on your best behavior. Yes, most of the guests at this party are usually people we've known for a long time and are practically family. People I trust.

Spending tonight with all the children though? It's been wonderful. And we're creating priceless memories they will never forget.

I love that.

"Come on." West hooks his arm around my shoulders and steers me around. "Let's go talk to your brother."

Whit really didn't like West at first. More like he didn't know him and therefore, he didn't trust him. It took a while but eventually my husband wore him down—and now it's like they're the best of friends, along with Spencer. Throw my cousin Crew into the mix, and they're all part of some Lancaster private men's club.

I'm just grateful they get along. And I love how Crew has become a regular part of our immediate family. The majority of our children are around the same age which made us all gravitate towards each other. It's nice.

They're not just my family, but it feels like we're friends too.

"Hot toddy?" Marta is approaching us, now carrying a tray full of delicious drinks of the adult variety.

"Definitely." West takes a cup downright eagerly before glancing over at me. "You want one?"

I start to shake my head but Marta doesn't even hesitate, handing a cup to me. "It'll warm your insides," she says before she bustles off. "I'll bring the champagne out in a minute!"

West is grinning at me from above the rim of his cup, just before he takes a sip. "Damn, it's strong."

"Lots of alcohol?" I take a sip, wincing. "Oh, most definitely."

"I bet she thinks we need it after spending the entire evening with the kids."

"They aren't so bad." I shrug.

"No, they aren't, are they?" West glances over at where Sylvie and Spence stand. "Is your sister feeling okay?"

I sneak a look in Sylvie's direction. She's laughing at something Wren is telling her and it's nice to see a smile on her face.

"You know how she can get when we spend any length of time in this house." I wasn't there the day Mother died, thank God, but it lingers in Sylvie's head to this day, which isn't a surprise. It's a shame that our mother can still have such a hold over her.

Though she's much better now—Sylvie. Being a mother has changed her for one. And then there's her steady prince, Spencer. He is the one person she can count on above all else. Spence loves my sister like no one else can, and for that, I'm eternally grateful to him.

"I don't blame her, though I'm glad Whit didn't sell the place." The look on West's face turns wistful. "Sometimes I have regret, selling the family business."

"It was the right thing to do," I reassure him as always. "And that was a long time ago. What's done is done."

I am not the type to regret much. There are seasons to life and though some are hard to let go, the future always brings with it good things. More opportunities. More growth. A deepening of relationships, especially with our children.

I love our girls. Paris and Pru are the lights of our lives and keep things interesting. And they're funny—they make me laugh constantly. They're sweet and total Daddy's girls, and I haven't pushed dancing on either one of them, which makes me proud.

Mother always pushed. And pushed and pushed and pushed some more. To the point that I was exhausted, all the time. I ran away from my family because I couldn't stand being around my parents for any length of time.

My children want to be with us. They actually enjoy spending time with us, and I love that. More than anything, I love them.

"We should buy a house out here. I hear the McLaughlin estate down the road is for sale," West suggests, his voice far too casual.

My brows shoot up. "You want to be neighbors with Whit and Summer?"

"I like it out here." West shrugs. "What do you think?"

We have our apartment and a house in the Hamptons that belonged to West's parents. Plus, we have a home in Napa that has been in West's family for generations. We're not interested in living in California though. That's too far from our family here.

"I actually don't mind the idea." My answer makes my husband smile. "We should schedule an appointment with the realtor and see what the house looks like inside."

"Already done." West is grinning. "We have an appointment on the second."

"Oh, you." I swat at his chest and he catches my hand, bringing it up to his mouth and delivering a kiss to my knuckles. "What if I told you that I wasn't interested?"

"I would've canceled the appointment." He shrugs. "But I know you, Carolina. I had a feeling you'd want to at least see it."

"You're right." I watch as he rubs his thumb across the ring he gave me so long ago. The one I still wear on my middle finger. "You know me so well."

"We have been together for a while," he says wryly.

"A few years," I say with a giggle.

And I never giggle.

He yanks me into his arms, delivering a sound kiss upon my lips. "I can't wait to count down the end of the year with you."

"Why?" I smooth my hand over his chest. He's wearing a suit like the rest of the men, but no tie, his shirt unbuttoned a little farther down than the rest. I like that he still does that. The man has swagger and it still catches my attention all these years later.

"I have a feeling the new year is going to bring plenty of good things," he murmurs, his head descending, his lips drawing closer to mine.

"Oh, it always does," I whisper, just as his lips brush mine. "Especially when we're together."

"Truer words were never spoken." He kisses me, stealing my breath. "I love you, Carolina."

"I love you too, Weston." My husband kisses me, swallowing whatever words I planned on saying.

They didn't matter anyway. What we just said to each other was enough.

SIX
IRIS

I WATCH Marta move about the room along with our butler Jerry, the both of them carrying trays laden with glasses full of champagne or sparkling apple cider. Marta is in charge of our glasses, and when she approaches us, handing off one to me and one to Willow, we both bow our heads to her with a smile, our *thank-you's* ringing together in unison.

Willow stares at the amber liquid in the glass so hard it looks like her eyes are crossing. "I sort of wished I could've sampled the champagne."

"No, you don't," Row pipes up as he joins us, clutching his own glass already. "It was kind of gross."

"How was it gross?" I ask, curious. I'm still thinking about what my father told me. How I shouldn't snitch on my brother all the time and I need to try and unite with him instead.

I just don't know how. When I tried to approach August earlier, he told me, and I quote, to fuck off.

Ugh, he's rude. Always cursing at me and Vaughn. I have a feeling he knows I'm the one who told on him sneaking the champagne and giving some to Rowan.

Oh well, I can't worry about it. Augie is always mad at me. I'm used to it by now.

"It was bitter." Row screws his face up, making me giggle. "And it sparkled on my tongue. Like bubbles."

"That sounds...nice," Willow says, a wistful expression on her face.

I don't remember life without Willow, and I like it that way. I asked Mom a long time ago if my cousin could be my best friend, and she said of course.

"Having someone you're related to who's also your best friend is the best. You can connect on so many levels," Mom said, her eyes glowing with happiness. "I'm just thrilled you two get along. When you were toddlers, you'd fight all the time and make each other cry."

I love hearing those stories about me and Willow making each other cry, I don't know why. They make me laugh.

"I don't like the bitter part," I say with all the authority I can muster. Like I know what I'm talking about. "I'll just stick with the cider, thanks."

I lift my glass in a toast, about to take a sip when Willow grabs my arm, preventing me from getting my lips on the rim of the glass.

"You can't drink it yet!" she practically shrieks.

I frown at her. "Why not?"

"It's bad luck. Do you want to put a curse on yourself for the next year?" I shake my head, my heart tripping over itself at the thought. "You can't take a drink until we all yell Happy New Year."

"I can wait." I set my glass on the nearby table and Willow does as well, along with Row. "What time is it anyway?"

"Ten minutes to midnight!" Mom shouts, and I realize she's been listening in on our conversation.

What if we'd been discussing something private? We live in this huge house yet my parents seem to know everything that's going on with us. Everything that's said. I love them. I love that we're all so close, but I'm starting to envy the distance they give to August whenever he seems to need it, which is pretty much all the time.

They always say he's a teenager and he needs his space. Well, guess what? I'm about to turn thirteen, which means I'm going to need some space too.

And plenty of it.

My parents start handing out party favors for all of us to use when the clock strikes twelve. Paper top hats and glitter tiaras. Gold and black feather boas and silly sunglasses. Poppers and noisemakers and tiny paper horns.

Willow and I wear matching tiaras and so do the twins, while the boys wear the black top hats and sunglasses. We all look ridiculous and the younger boys won't stop blowing into the shiny gold horns but I don't even mind. We're having too much fun, anticipation filling the room as we get closer to midnight.

Dad turns on the TV and finds a New Year's show. They're live in Times Square and our cousin's husband Tate Ramsey is singing one of his latest hits.

"Look, there's Scarlett!" Mom yells, pointing at the screen.

Scarlett is standing off to the side of the stage, a proud smile on her face as she watches Tate perform. I wonder what it's like, being married to a famous pop star.

Every time we see them though, they're so perfectly normal, it's hard to believe he's famous.

Once Tate is done singing, the camera switches to the glittering ball that sits high above Times Square. It slowly descends as the time speeds by on the digital clock that's shown on the top right corner of the TV.

"Get ready, everyone!" Wren tells us and we all surround the TV, our gazes never straying from the gold ball on the television.

"This is exactly what I used to do when I was a kid with my mother," Mom says as she slips in between me and Willow. "We'd watch the ball drop too."

"Some things never change," I tell her and her smile turns almost sad.

"I suppose you're right." She grabs my hand and kisses my cheek. "I love you, sweetie."

"I love you too." My gaze goes to the screen because I can't help it. I'm too excited.

"You going to make a wish?" Willow asks me after Mom leaves us to go stand with Dad.

"A wish? On what?" I'm confused. I don't think we've ever made a wish on New Year's Eve before.

"When the clock hits midnight, let's take a drink and make a wish for what we want in the new year." Willow smiles. "Maybe that'll help it come true."

"It can't hurt," I say with a shrug.

"Can I make a wish?" Row asks, right as August approaches us.

"Of course, you can," I tell him, Willow nodding her agreement.

"You guys are lame," August mutters, rolling his eyes.

"At least we're not mean like you," I throw at him. Wanting to prove I can dish it out just like he does.

"I'm not mean." He actually seems insulted.

Row says nothing. Willow giggles, covering her mouth with her fingers to stop it.

"You are so mean. Maybe that'll be my wish this year. That my brother will be nicer to all of us," I say.

"Good luck with that happening," Willow murmurs, laughing when Augie sends her an annoyed look. "See? You can't help yourself, Augie."

"Whatever. And don't call me that." He stomps off, mad like usual.

Ugh, I can't worry about him.

"We're definitely making a wish at midnight," I tell Willow and Row. "And I'm not wasting mine on him."

"Good," Willow says with a nod, her gaze going to the TV screen. "Oh no, we need to get ready!"

The countdown is on. The younger kids start counting down from fifty, which is irritating but the parents seem into it. They start counting too.

I only join in at twenty, clutching the glass in my hand, spinning the noisemaker with my other hand. The noise in the room grows louder and louder and when we hit ten, I close my eyes and come up with a wish.

It hits me right when we hit two, and I open my eyes, screaming "one" as loud as I can.

HAPPY NEW YEAR!!!

We're screaming and yelling and carrying on. The adults are kissing their significant others, and I take a big gulp from my glass to toast the New Year, thinking about my wish.

"What did you wish for?" Row asks minutes later, after we've gone quieter.

"It won't come true if we tell," Willow chastises. "Right, Iris?"

"Definitely." I nod, though I'm dying to tell them what mine is.

I wished we'd have this party every year. Just us. Just the family and no one else.

I hope it comes true.

SEVEN
ARCH

"WE'RE NEVER GOING to make it." I keep my gaze fixed on the road, but it's tough when there's so much snow falling from the sky that it makes it hard to see. The windshield wipers are whipping back and forth across the glass at a tremendous speed, but they're not really helping. And all the cars on the freeway—not that there are many—are creeping along, afraid they might slide or get stuck.

"Maybe we should turn back," my wife says, patting her giant belly.

I glance over at her, pride filling me as it always does when I see how heavy she is with my child. She's going to give birth at any minute. It was probably a stupid idea to try and drive out to my cousin's house for a New Year's Eve party in the middle of a snowstorm.

There's no probably about it. It's an awful idea.

"We can stop at a hotel," I suggest. "There are some at the next exit I think."

Daisy nibbles on her lower lip, staring straight ahead. Her brows are drawn together in worry and I feel like an ass for insisting we try and get to Whit and Summer's house tonight, thinking we could beat the storm. That didn't work out. "I think that's a good idea."

She winces the moment the words leave her, clutching the bottom of her belly in a way that fills me with alarm.

"What's wrong?"

"Nothing." She exhales, leaning back against her seat. "Just a cramp."

"A cramp, my ass," I mutter as I hit the blinker and pull off on the exit, thankful to see a towering building looming up ahead. I'm sure that's a hotel and we're going to be in it in approximately five minutes, if not sooner. "Are you going into labor?"

"Of course not." She sounds insulted, and I can't help but smile. "This child of ours is coming in January."

This child is a Lancaster, which means he is impatient and eager to make his debut to the world. Maybe even right now. We waited a few years after we got married to try for a baby and the minute that we stopped using birth control, Daisy became pregant.

I'm grateful it was so easy. I can't wait to meet this son of mine. And when Daisy's ready, I want to try for another one.

And another one after that.

I carefully pull into the mostly cleared drive of the hotel, pleased to see a bellman running toward my wife's car door when I put the vehicle in park. I climb out of the car in a hurry, thankful there's a roof above us so we're not getting pelted with heavy snow, and rush over to Daisy, taking her arm so both the bellman and I can assist her into the building.

"I'm not an invalid," she gently chastises me with a smile. "I can walk on my own."

"I don't want you falling," I say, tightening my hold on her arm.

"The ground is slippery, ma'am," the bellman tacks on.

"Thank you," Daisy breathes once we're in the warm lobby. Gentle piano plays in the background and there's no one inside save for a few employees behind the counter.

I arrange for a room while Daisy rests in an overstuffed chair. The bellman even brings her a glass of water, which she takes from him with a pleasant smile on her face. My wife is still sunshine on a cold, dark day and I love it when she shares that brightness with others.

But she saves most of it just for me.

"We're on the ground floor," I tell her once I've paid for everything and got our keys. I offer her my hand and she takes it so I can haul her to her feet. "They're bringing our luggage to the room."

"Make sure you give him a good tip." She inclines her head toward the bellman who helped her. "He's so nice."

"Will do." I keep her hand locked in mine and lead her to the corridor where our hotel room is.

"Why aren't we on a higher floor?"

"I didn't want to have to wait for an elevator in case you go into labor," I admit, mentally reading off the room numbers as we walk past them. How far down this hall do we have to go anyway?

"Oh Arch. I already told you I'm not going into labor."

I stop in front of room 188 and wave the key in front of the screen, the light turning green immediately. I open the door and step aside, letting Daisy enter first before I stride in after her, the door slamming behind us.

"It's nice," she says as she waddles around the room, wincing every couple of steps. "What will we do for dinner though? I'm already hungry."

She's been hungry this entire pregnancy and I knew she'd say that.

"They have room service. I asked."

She frowns. "I'm sorry we didn't get to go to your cousin's house for New Year's."

"It's okay. I didn't want to party with a bunch of old people any way." I go to the window and peek outside. The snow is coming down in endless white sheets. I'm glad we didn't continue on. We could've got stuck out there.

Daisy laughs. "They're not old."

"They're older than us." I turn to study her. She's got her hand on her belly again, another wince on her face and I rush toward her, running both of my hands on her belly. "You're definitely going into labor."

"No, I'm not. You need to stop panicking about it." She offers me a reassuring smile. "It's like you want me to go into labor and have your baby in the middle of a hotel room."

"Better than the car." I press my hand firmly against her tight belly, pleased to feel movement beneath my palm. "This guy never stops moving."

"I know. It's nonstop. Like his daddy."

"I hope he looks like you."

"I don't." She shakes her head. "I want him to be the spitting image of his father."

Our son gives my hand a resounding kick. "I feel like Mary and Joseph right now, tucked away at the inn."

"Seriously? You're getting your holidays confused." More laughter. "First of all, that's Christmas. And second, I am definitely not a virgin."

"You've got that right." I kiss her, my lips lingering on hers, my hand still on her belly. I can't get close to her like I want to, her belly is so big. "I love you, Daze."

"I love you too." Her lips linger on mine when she asks, "Did you text Whit and let him know we can't make it?"

"I'll do that right now." I deliver another kiss. "We can make our own party tonight. Ring in the new year together. Just the three of us."

"I like the way that sounds," she admits. "The three of us. A family of three."

"If I had my choice, we'll eventually be a family of...six."

Her eyes go wide. "You want four children?"

"Maybe more?" I shrug. "It'll be fun."

"Right, because you're not the one giving birth to them." She rests her hand on her belly once more and I settle my hand on top of hers. "Let's see how it goes with the first one."

I smile, my chest tight. God, I love this woman. "Sounds like a plan."

EPILOGUE
WREN

NEW YEAR'S *Day*

"Well?" My husband wraps me up in his strong arms, pulling on me until I'm lying practically on top of him. It's many hours past midnight and the house has long gone quiet. "Was it a good New Year's Eve for you?"

I told him a long time ago that I never liked this holiday. That it always made me sad and I was never exactly sure why. Since that confession, my husband has made it his mission every year to make this day the best possible. Sometimes even better than my birthday, which is on Christmas.

And he always does it well. This year is no exception.

"Yes," I murmur, tilting my head back in the hopes that he'll kiss me.

He does, just like I knew he would.

"Even partying with the children?" he whispers against my lips.

"Oh, that was the best part." I kiss him, my lips lingering. "We should do that every year. Forget inviting anyone else and keep it a family affair."

"That sounds nice," he says.

"I agree. I think the kids would like it too. They had so much fun. I loved seeing their faces light up with excitement when we told them they were invited to the party."

"They've been watching us for years."

"I wish Arch and Daisy could've made it," I say after a few minutes of silence.

"I'm just glad they're safe in a hotel," Crew says. "She's about to have that baby."

"I know." Another baby in the family. I love all the babies. The children. I love witnessing them grow and thrive and enjoy their time together. It's so nice, to have a large, close family. I didn't have that as a kid and I'm grateful we can give that to our children.

We lie there in each other's arms for a moment, my eyes falling closed. It's been a long day and I'm sleepy but apparently my husband isn't.

"You know, we used to watch our parents here when I was a kid. Though we'd spy on them by hiding behind a door and peeking around the corner. They had the party in the ballroom," Crew says.

"I'm sure it was beautiful."

"So many people. Sylvia always knew how to throw a party."

"Whit and Summer do too. And their parties I'm sure are better," I say firmly, not about to speak nicely about a woman who essentially tortured her daughter her entire life. I can't imagine what that must've been like. And I can't even wrap my head around doing something like that to Willow or my boys. They're all my precious babies. I could never harm a hair on their heads.

"Their parties are definitely better," Crew agrees, kissing me yet again. "We should go to sleep."

"You're the one who keeps talking," I point out.

He chuckles. "You're right. I'll be quiet."

"Good." I snuggle closer, my eyes closing again when he says one more thing.

"Happy New Year's Day, Birdy."

"Happy New Year's, Crew."

"I love you," he whispers.

"I love you too."

CAN'T GET ENOUGH of the Lancasters? The next gen series is coming in 2024, kicking off with Willow Lancaster's story June 4th! Keep scrolling to read this exclusive excerpt from All My Kisses For You!

ALL MY KISSES FOR YOU SNEAK PEEK!

Prologue
Crew

She approaches me slowly, her tiny feet shuffling across the bare wood floor, her long, dark hair, so like her mother's, tumbling past her shoulders in a haphazard mess. I know for a fact Wren brushes our daughter's hair after a bath every night. If she's not doing it, I am.

Somehow, our sweet Willow makes a mess of it in those twilight minutes between bath and bed. Every single time.

"Daddy." Her big blue eyes that match mine shine up at me, her little rosebud lips pursed into a perfect pout. She is truly the most beautiful little girl in the entire world, but I'm her father so I'm biased. "Can you put me to bed?"

I glance over at my wife, who's standing in the doorway of the living room, a soft smile on her face, cradling our baby boy in her arms. Another Lancaster to carry on the family name.

Just performing our expected duties, I said to Wren when she told me she was pregnant. She rolled her eyes and gave me a gentle shove which caused me to pull her down onto our bed and perform more of those duties on her...

But I digress.

"I thought you asked Mama to put you to bed." I'm already rising to my feet, holding my hand out to our daughter and she takes it, curling her small fingers around mine.

"I want you instead," Willow says firmly.

Wren crosses her arms in front of her, her expression a little weary. Our son is keeping her up at night because he's always hungry and she's breastfeeding. "She specifically requested her daddy."

"I don't mind." I stop beside my wife, leaning in to brush a kiss to her cheek before I murmur close to her ear, "Are you feeling all right?"

She nods. "A little tired. Row is finally asleep."

Our son. Rowan. He doesn't like to take naps and isn't the best sleeper in general. Wren says it's because he never wants to miss a thing and I tend to agree with her.

"Go to bed." I deliver another kiss, this time to her lips. "I'll join you in a few minutes."

"After you tell me a story," Willow demands.

We go to her bedroom, the light on her nightstand already on, as well as the light we installed to highlight Wren's favorite art piece, which still resides in this room. I tuck Willow into her fluffy princess dream of a bed, brushing her dark hair from her eyes and she scoots away from me, patting the empty spot beside her.

"Sit."

I do as she says because this little girl owns my heart like her mother does and settle in beside her, slipping my arm around her slender shoulders and scooping her closer to me. She tilts her head back so our eyes meet, her lips parting and I have a feeling what her request is going to be.

"Tell me the story about you and Mama."

My gaze goes to the piece hanging on the wall, smiling as the memories wash over me, one after another. Willow has already heard this story countless times and she's barely three. But she can't get enough of it.

"Where shall I start?" I ask.

"When Mama didn't like you." Willow wrinkles her nose then bursts out laughing. "It's funny."

"That would make you laugh." I tickle her and she giggles uncontrollably, so loud that Wren calls from our bedroom.

"What's going on back there?"

We both go silent, sharing a secret look and I press my finger to Willow's lips.

"Nothing. I was just telling her a story," I respond.

"Uh huh." The doubt in my wife's voice is obvious and I smile.

So does Willow.

"We need to be quiet," I whisper.

"Don't tickle me," Willow says, sounding completely logical.

My girl is smart. Much like her mama.

Clearing my throat, I lean against the headboard and stare at the art piece, telling the story about watching for Wren every day before school started. How I didn't know her but I wanted to, but she never wanted to give me the time of day. How we were forced to work together on a school project and we slowly got to know each other.

And swiftly fell in love.

"What about the kisses?" Willow stares at the piece with me.

"What about them?"

"You owe her two million." She remembers that. She remembers pretty much every detail of our story. "How many do you give her?"

"A lot."

"How many?"

"We're probably only a quarter of the way in," I say, and my poor little daughter frowns, confusion etched in her delicate features. "Let's just say Daddy still owes Mama a lot of kisses."

The frown disappears, just like that. "I want kisses."

I give her one on her forehead. Her nose. Each cheek. "All the kisses you could ever want, you deserve."

"I wanna husband who gives me kisses too." Her gaze turns dreamy as she stares at the art piece once more.

Over my dead body, is what I want to say, thinking of my own self not too long ago, and how completely over the top I was.

How badly I wanted Wren and went after her with a dogged determination that still surprises me. I've never chased after something like I chased after Wren.

And look at me now. I got her. I love her. I love our little and I love our son. Life is pretty great.

"Someday," I tell Willow, dropping another kiss on top of her head. "But for now, save your kisses for your mama and daddy. And your brother."

"Okay." She tilts her head back to look at me, and for a moment I think she looks older. Wiser than she should. "But someday I'm going to kiss someone else. Like Mama kisses you."

"Uh, sure." I swallow hard, hating the thought of her being so grown up. She's still my baby. My first child. My daughter. "Just…don't give your kisses away too easily."

She frowns. "Doesn't everyone need a kiss?"

I say nothing, unsure of how to explain myself. She's unreasonable a lot of the time but she's still a toddler so it's expected. She's also naturally fiery and hot headed—Wren calls that the Lancaster in her.

She's right. I can't deny it.

"Kisses are the best. They're so pretty." She turns toward the art, a little sigh escaping her. "I want it."

"Want what?"

"Kisses." She turns a toothy grin on me. "Lots of them."

Shit.

I'm in trouble.

Want to read more? Preorder All My Kisses For You, coming June 4th to the US and Canada!

UPCOMING RELEASES

Coming January 30th, 2024 (reissue)

Crave & Torn

Coming February 6th, 2024

Lonely for You Only

Coming March 5th, 2024

The Liars Club

Coming April 23rd, 2024 (reissue)

Savor & Intoxicated

Coming June 4th, 2024

All My Kisses For You

ALSO BY MONICA MURPHY

Lancaster Prep

Things I Wanted To Say (but never did)
A Million Kisses in Your Lifetime
Birthday Kisses
Promises We Meant to Keep
I'll Always Be With You
You Said I Was Your Favorite

The Players

Playing Hard to Get
Playing by The Rules
Playing to Win

Wedded Bliss (Lancaster)

The Reluctant Bride
The Ruthless Groom
The Reckless Union
The Arranged Marriage boxset

College Years

The Freshman
The Sophomore
The Junior
The Senior

Dating Series

Save The Date
Fake Date
Holidate
Hate to Date You
Rate A Date
Wedding Date
Blind Date

The Callahans

Close to Me
Falling For Her
Addicted To Him
Meant To Be
Fighting For You
Making Her Mine
A Callahan Wedding

Forever Yours Series

You Promised Me Forever
Thinking About You
Nothing Without You

Damaged Hearts Series

Her Defiant Heart
His Wasted Heart
Damaged Hearts

Friends Series

Just Friends
More Than Friends
Forever

The Never Duet

Never Tear Us Apart
Never Let You Go

The Rules Series

Fair Game
In The Dark
Slow Play

Safe Bet

The Fowler Sisters Series

Owning Violet
Stealing Rose
Taming Lily

Reverie Series

His Reverie
Her Destiny

Billionaire Bachelors Club Series

Crave
Torn
Savor
Intoxicated

One Week Girlfriend Series

One Week Girlfriend
Second Chance Boyfriend
Three Broken Promises
Drew + Fable Forever
Four Years Later
Five Days Until You

A Drew + Fable Christmas

Standalone YA Titles

Daring The Bad Boy

Saving It

Pretty Dead Girls

ABOUT THE AUTHOR

Monica Murphy is a New York Times, USA Today and international bestselling author. Her books have been translated in almost a dozen languages and have sold millions of copies worldwide. Both a traditionally published and independently published author, she writes young adult and new adult romance, as well as contemporary romance and women's fiction. She's also known as USA Today bestselling author Karen Erickson.

- facebook.com/MonicaMurphyAuthor
- instagram.com/monicamurphyauthor
- bookbub.com/profile/monica-murphy
- goodreads.com/monicamurphyauthor
- amazon.com/Monica-Murphy/e/B00AVPYIGG
- pinterest.com/msmonicamurphy
- tiktok.com/@monicamurphyauthor